(LG) JVP

BEATRIX POTTER
COLLECTION

BEATRIX POTTER

F. WARNE & Co

FREDERICK WARNE
Published by the Penguin Group
Penguin Books Ltd, 80 Strand, London WC2R 0RL, England
Penguin Young Readers Group, 345 Hudson Street, New York, New York 10014, USA
Penguin (Group) Australia, 250 Camberwell Road, Camberwell, Victoria 3124, Australia
Penguin Group (NZ), cnr Airborne and Rosedale Roads, Albany, Auckland 1310,
New Zealand
A Penguin Company

BEATRIX POTTER COLLECTION

BEATRIX POTTER

F. WARNE & CO

Contents

Peter Rabbit

Naughty Peter Rabbit finds himself in all kinds
of trouble as he squeezes himself under the gate
into Mr. McGregor's garden.

Tom Kitten

Mrs. Tabitha Twitchit dresses her three kittens before
tea in their best clothes. But mischievous Tom and his
two sisters are not going to stay clean for long.

Jemima Puddle-Duck

As Jemima Puddle-duck tries to find a convenient
nesting place, she meets a mysterious whiskered
gentleman. Watch out Jemima, can you trust him?

Benjamin Bunny

When Benjamin Bunny finds that his cousin, Peter,
has lost his clothes in Mr. McGregor's garden, he
decides they must go to retrieve them.

Nursery Rhymes

Beatrix Potter's exquisite sketches and watercolours
perfectly complement this collection of traditional
rhymes and riddles.

FREDERICK WARNE
Published by the Penguin Group
Penguin Books Ltd, 80 Strand, London WC2R 0RL, England
Penguin Young Readers Group, 345 Hudson Street, New York, New York 10014, USA
Penguin (Group) Australia, 250 Camberwell Road, Camberwell, Victoria 3124, Australia
Penguin Group (NZ), cnr Airborne and Rosedale Roads, Albany, Auckland 1310,
New Zealand
A Penguin Company

1 3 5 7 9 10 8 6 4 2
Copyright © Frederick Warne & Co., 2006

1 3 5 7 9 10 8 6 4 2

New reproductions of Beatrix Potter's book illustrations copyright © Frederick Warne & Co.,
2002
Original text and illustrations copyright © Frederick Warne & Co., 1902

Additional illustrations by Colin Twinn and Alex Vining

Frederick Warne & Co. is the owner of all rights, copyrights and trademarks in the Beatrix
Potter character names and illustrations.

THE TALE OF PETER RABBIT

A SIMPLIFIED RETELLING OF THE ORIGINAL TALE BY
BEATRIX POTTER

This is Peter Rabbit.

He lives here with his
mother, Mrs. Rabbit, and
his sisters, Flopsy, Mopsy
and Cotton-tail.

One morning Mrs. Rabbit said, "I am going out, children. Now run along, but don't go into Mr. McGregor's garden."

Then Mrs. Rabbit took her
basket and her umbrella and
walked through the wood.

Flopsy, Mopsy and
Cotton-tail were good
little rabbits. They went
to pick blackberries.

But Peter was a naughty little rabbit. He ran to Mr. McGregor's garden and squeezed under the gate!

Peter sat in the garden and ate lots of radishes.

Then, feeling rather sick, he went to look for some parsley to make him feel better.

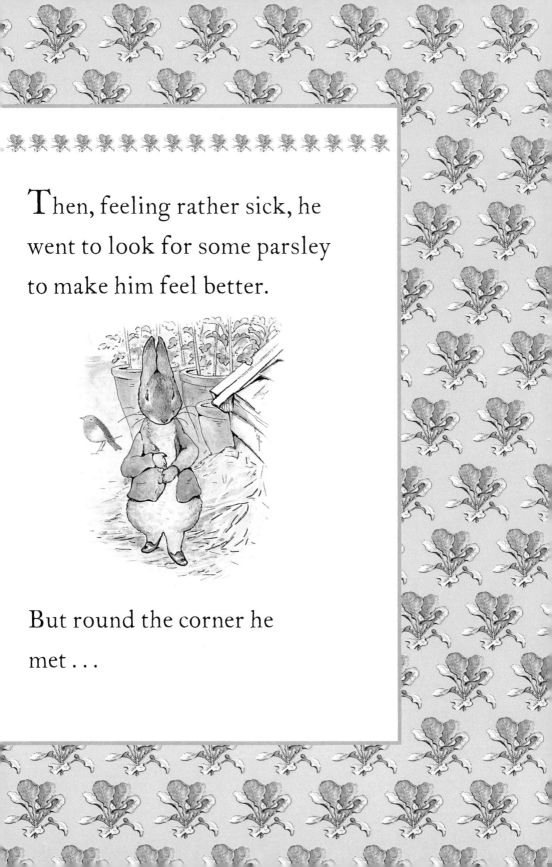

But round the corner he met . . .

... Mr. McGregor!

Mr. McGregor ran after Peter Rabbit, waving a rake and shouting, "Stop thief!"

Peter ran into a net and got caught by the buttons on his blue jacket.

Then Mr. McGregor tried
to trap Peter with a sieve!

Peter wriggled out but he
lost his jacket and shoes.

Peter jumped into a watering-can.

Mr. McGregor was looking for him underneath the flowerpots.

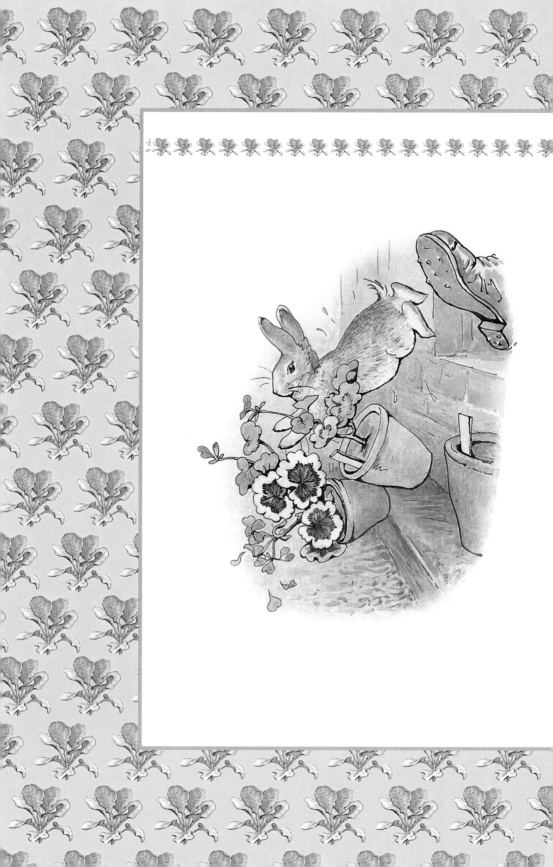

Then Peter jumped out
of a window and knocked
over some flowerpots.
He got away!

Mr. McGregor was tired
of running after Peter.

He went back to his work.

Peter heard the *scritch*, *scratch* of Mr. McGregor's hoe. He climbed on to a wheelbarrow and looked across the garden.

He could see the gate!

P eter ran as fast as he
could go. Mr. McGregor
saw him but Peter didn't
care. He slipped under the
gate and was safe at last.

When Peter got home, he was so tired that he flopped down on to the floor.

Mrs. Rabbit was cooking. "Where have you been, Peter Rabbit?" she said.

Peter Rabbit was not very
well. Mrs. Rabbit put him to
bed and made him some tea.

But Flopsy, Mopsy and
Cotton-tail had bread
and milk and blackberries
for supper.

FREDERICK WARNE
Published by the Penguin Group
Penguin Books Ltd, 80 Strand, London WC2R 0RL, England
Penguin Young Readers Group, 345 Hudson Street, New York, New York 10014, USA
Penguin (Group) Australia, 250 Camberwell Road, Camberwell, Victoria 3124, Australia
Penguin Group (NZ), cnr Airborne and Rosedale Roads, Albany, Auckland 1310,
New Zealand
A Penguin Company

1 3 5 7 9 10 8 6 4 2
Copyright © Frederick Warne & Co., 2006

1 3 5 7 9 10 8 6 4 2

The Tale of
Tom Kitten

A SIMPLIFIED RETELLING OF THE ORIGINAL TALE BY
BEATRIX POTTER

Here are three little
kittens: Mittens,
Tom Kitten and Moppet.

One day their mother,
Mrs. Tabitha Twitchit, took
them indoors to get ready
for a tea-party.

First she scrubbed their faces. (This kitten is Moppet.)

Then she brushed their fur. (This kitten is Mittens.)

Then she combed their tails
and whiskers. (This kitten is
Tom.)

Mrs. Tabitha Twitchit took
some fine clothes out of the
drawer and dressed her kittens.

The kittens found the clothes
very uncomfortable.
Moppet and Mittens wore
white pinafores.

Tom Kitten's blue suit
was too small for him.
The buttons burst off.

Mrs. Tabitha Twitchit
sewed them on again.

When they were ready,
Mrs. Tabitha Twitchit sent
them outside to play.

"Keep your frocks clean,
children," she said.

In the garden, Tom Kitten
chased a butterfly.

Moppet and Mittens fell
down on the path and made
their clothes dirty.

Then Moppet and Mittens climbed up and sat on the garden wall. "Come along, Tom," they called.

Tom Kitten's buttons had
burst off again.

Moppet and Mittens
helped Tom to climb up the
garden wall.

He lost his hat and his suit was
falling off.

As the kittens sat on the garden wall, three ducks came walking along the road. They were called the Puddle-ducks.

The Puddle-ducks put on
Tom's hat.

Moppet, Mittens and Tom
Kitten laughed so much that
they fell off the garden wall.

"Will you help us dress Tom
Kitten?" said Moppet to the
Puddle-ducks.

But one of the Puddle-ducks
put Tom Kitten's clothes
on himself!

"It is a very fine morning,"
said the Puddle-duck.

Then the three Puddle-ducks
walked off along the road
with all of the kittens' clothes.

Their feet went *pit pat,
paddle pat! Pit pat, waddle pat!*

Mrs. Tabitha Twitchit
found her kittens sitting
on the garden wall with
no clothes on.

She was very angry.
She smacked those kittens,
and sent them upstairs!

When Mrs. Tabitha's friends arrived, she told them that her kittens were in bed with the measles.

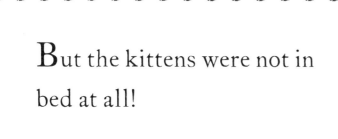

But the kittens were not in
bed at all!

The Puddle-ducks went into a pond and the clothes all came off. They are still looking for them!

FREDERICK WARNE
Published by the Penguin Group
Penguin Books Ltd, 80 Strand, London WC2R 0RL, England
Penguin Young Readers Group, 345 Hudson Street, New York, New York 10014, USA
Penguin (Group) Australia, 250 Camberwell Road, Camberwell, Victoria 3124, Australia
Penguin Group (NZ), cnr Airborne and Rosedale Roads, Albany, Auckland 1310,
New Zealand
A Penguin Company

1 3 5 7 9 10 8 6 4 2
Copyright © Frederick Warne & Co., 2006

1 3 5 7 9 10 8 6 4 2

New reproductions of Beatrix Potter's book illustrations copyright © Frederick Warne & Co.,
2002
Original text and illustrations copyright © Frederick Warne & Co., 1908

Additional illustrations by Colin Twinn and Alex Vining

Frederick Warne & Co. is the owner of all rights, copyrights and trademarks in the Beatrix
Potter character names and illustrations.

THE TALE OF
JEMIMA PUDDLE-DUCK

A SIMPLIFIED RETELLING OF THE ORIGINAL TALE BY
BEATRIX POTTER

This is the story of Jemima Puddle-duck.

Jemima lived on a farm. She wanted to hatch her own eggs but the farmer's wife would not let her.

Jemima's sister, Rebeccah, did not want to hatch her own eggs.

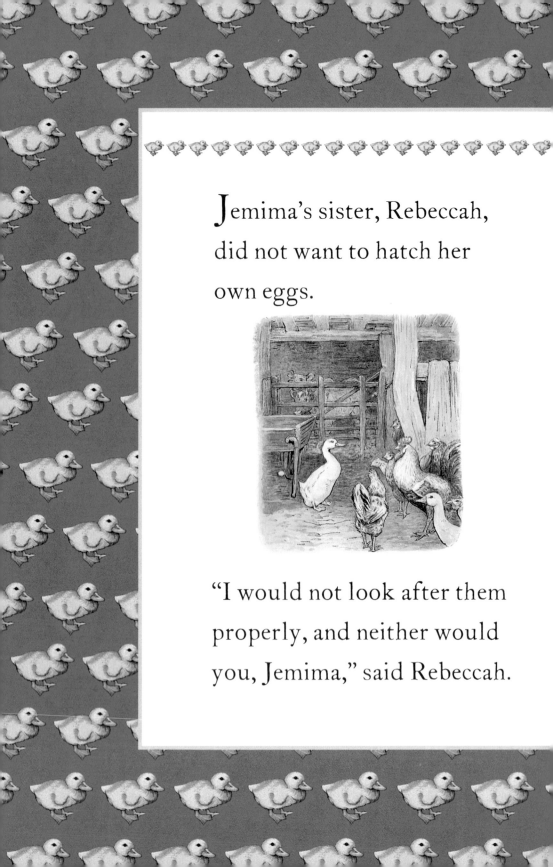

"I would not look after them properly, and neither would you, Jemima," said Rebeccah.

Jemima tried to hide her
eggs so that she could look
after them.

But Jemima's eggs were always
taken away from her.

One day Jemima left the farm so she could lay her eggs.

She wore a blue bonnet and a pink shawl.

Jemima Puddle-duck ran
down the hill and then
jumped off into the air.

She flew over the tree-tops
looking for a place to land.

Jemima landed in the wood and saw someone reading a newspaper.

"Quack?" said Jemima.

The gentleman looked at
Jemima. "Have you lost
your way?" he said.

Jemima told the gentleman
that she was trying to find
a place to lay her eggs.

The gentleman said,
"I have a shed. You may lay
your eggs in there."

He opened the door and
let Jemima in.

The shed was full of feathers.
It was very comfortable
and soft. Jemima Puddle-duck
made a nest.

She laid nine eggs.

The next day, the gentleman
said to Jemima, "Let us have
a dinner party."

"Bring some herbs from
the farm and I will make an
omelette."

Jemima met Kep.
He knew those herbs were
for cooking roast duck!

Kep ran to the village and
told the puppies.

Jemima went back to
the wood and found
the gentleman.

He spoke in an angry voice. "Check your eggs and then come into my house. Quickly!"

Jemima felt afraid.

Kep and the puppies found
the shed in the wood. They
shut Jemima in the shed to
keep her safe.

Then they chased the
gentleman away.
He never came back.

Kep opened the door of
the shed and let Jemima
Puddle-duck out.

Then Kep and the puppies
took Jemima back to the farm.

Jemima laid some more eggs and she was allowed to hatch them herself. She had four yellow ducklings.

FREDERICK WARNE
Published by the Penguin Group
Penguin Books Ltd, 80 Strand, London WC2R 0RL, England
Penguin Young Readers Group, 345 Hudson Street, New York, New York 10014, USA
Penguin (Group) Australia, 250 Camberwell Road, Camberwell, Victoria 3124, Australia
Penguin Group (NZ), cnr Airborne and Rosedale Roads, Albany, Auckland 1310,
New Zealand
A Penguin Company

1 3 5 7 9 10 8 6 4 2
Copyright © Frederick Warne & Co., 2006

1 3 5 7 9 10 8 6 4 2
This presentation first published by Ladybird Books Ltd, 2006
New reproductions of Beatrix Potter's book illustrations copyright © Frederick Warne & Co.,
2002
Original text and illustrations copyright © Frederick Warne & Co., 1904

Additional illustrations by Colin Twinn and Alex Vining

Frederick Warne & Co. is the owner of all rights, copyrights and trademarks in the Beatrix
Potter character names and illustrations.

THE TALE OF
BENJAMIN BUNNY

A SIMPLIFIED RETELLING OF THE ORIGINAL TALE BY
BEATRIX POTTER

This is the tale of
Benjamin Bunny.

One morning he sat on a bank
in the woods.

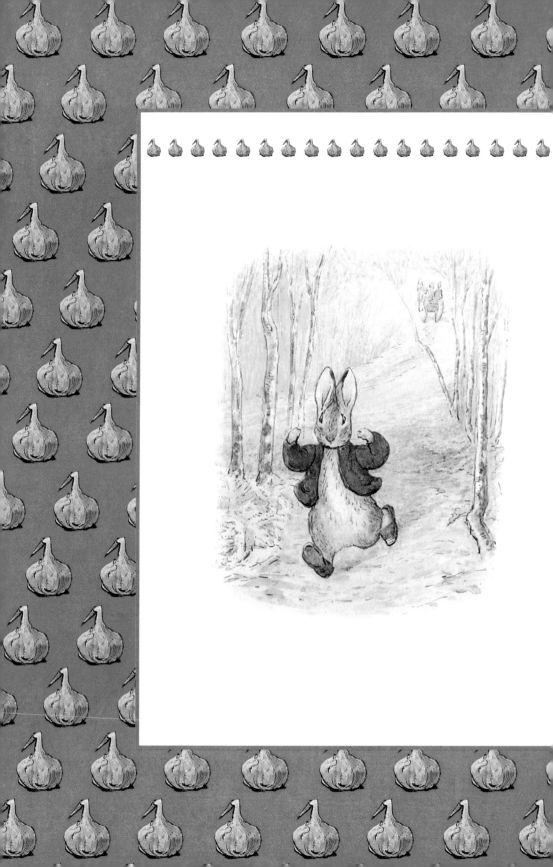

Benjamin Bunny saw a cart on the road. Mr. and Mrs. McGregor were in the cart. They were going out for the day.

Benjamin ran off to tell his cousin, Peter Rabbit.

As he peered behind a tree, Benjamin saw two little ears sticking out.

It was his cousin, Peter Rabbit, wrapped in a red handkerchief.

Benjamin sat beside Peter.
"Peter, who has got your
clothes?"

Peter told him that he had been chased round the garden by Mr. McGregor and had dropped his coat and shoes.

Mr. McGregor was using them for a scarecrow!

"Come along, Peter," said Benjamin. "Mr. and Mrs. McGregor have gone out in their cart. Let us go and find your clothes."

Benjamin and Peter stood
on the garden wall.

They could see Peter's shoes
and coat on the scarecrow.
There was a big green hat on
the scarecrow too.

Benjamin and Peter climbed
down a pear tree into the
garden. Peter fell down ...
but he was not hurt.

Peter put on his blue coat and Benjamin put on the green hat. It was much too big for him!

Then Benjamin and Peter
collected onions for Peter's
mother. They put them in
the red handkerchief.

As they walked through the
garden, Benjamin munched
on a lettuce leaf.

But Peter Rabbit felt very scared in Mr. McGregor's garden. He was so scared that he dropped the onions.

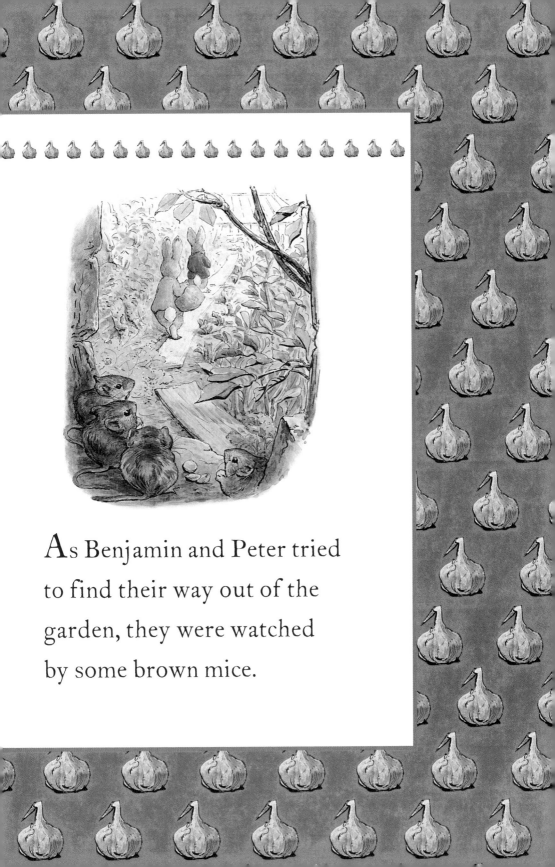

As Benjamin and Peter tried
to find their way out of the
garden, they were watched
by some brown mice.

Suddenly, the little
rabbits stopped . . .

This is what they saw—
a cat!

They hid underneath a
basket. The cat walked over
to the basket and . . .

She sat down on top of it!

The cat sat there for
a very long time. Benjamin
and Peter were very scared.

On the wall above the cat, Benjamin's father, old Mr. Bunny, was smoking a pipe. He was looking for his son.

Old Mr. Bunny jumped down from the wall and pushed the cat off the basket.

Then he took the red handkerchief of onions and marched those naughty rabbits home.

That night, the onions were hung in the kitchen, and Peter and his sister, Cotton-tail, folded up the red handkerchief.

Beatrix Potter was incredibly fond of rhymes.
These poems are from the 1905 and 1917 Appley
Dapply collections, rhymes from Cecily
Parsley collection, and verses from
some of her tales.

FREDERICK WARNE
Published by the Penguin Group
Penguin Books Ltd, 80 Strand, London WC2R 0RL, England
Penguin Young Readers Group, 345 Hudson Street, New York, New York 10014, USA
Penguin (Group) Australia, 250 Camberwell Road, Camberwell, Victoria 3124, Australia
Penguin Group (NZ), cnr Airborne and Rosedale Roads, Albany, Auckland 1310,
New Zealand
A Penguin Company

1 3 5 7 9 10 8 6 4 2
Copyright © Frederick Warne & Co., 2006

1 3 5 7 9 10 8 6 4 2

New reproductions of Beatrix Potter's book illustrations copyright © Frederick Warne & Co.,
2002
Original text and illustrations copyright © Frederick Warne & Co., 1905, 1910, 1913, 1917,
1922,

Frederick Warne & Co. is the owner of all rights, copyrights and trademarks in the Beatrix
Potter character names and illustrations.

BEATRIX POTTER
NURSERY RHYMES

BEATRIX POTTER

The old woman
who lived in a shoe

You know the old woman
 who lived in a shoe?
And had so many children
 she didn't know what to do?

I think if she lived
 in a little shoe-house–
That little old woman
 was surely a mouse!

Diggory Diggory Delvet

Diggory Diggory Delvet!
A little old man in black velvet;
He digs and he delves –
You can see for yourselves
The mounds dug by Diggory Delvet.

Old Mr Pricklepin

Old Mr Pricklepin
    has never a cushion to
    stick his pins in,
His nose is black and his
    beard is grey,
And he lives in an ash stump
    over the way.

To Market! To Market!

To Market! To Market!
Now isn't this funny?
You've got a basket,
And I've got some money!
– We went to market
And I spent my money,
Home again! home again!
Little Miss Bunny!

Tabitha Twitchit
is grown so fine

Tabitha Twitchit
is grown so fine
She lies in bed
until half past nine.
She breakfasts on muffins,
and eggs and ham,
And dines on red-herrings
and rasp-berry jam!!

If acorn-cups
were tea-cups

If acorn -cups were tea-cups,
what should we have to drink?
Why! honey-dew for sugar,
in a cuckoo-pint of milk;

With pats of witches' butter
and a tansey cake, I think,
Laid out upon a toad-stool
on a cloth of cob-web silk!

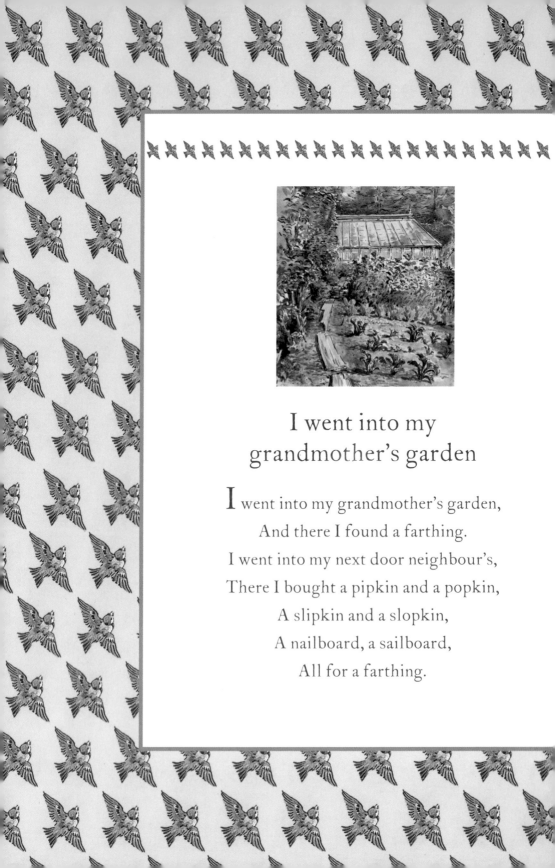

I went into my grandmother's garden

I went into my grandmother's garden,
And there I found a farthing.
I went into my next door neighbour's,
There I bought a pipkin and a popkin,
A slipkin and a slopkin,
A nailboard, a sailboard,
All for a farthing.

Kadiddle,
kadiddle, kadiddle

Kadddle, kadiddle, kadiddle!
Come dance to my dear little fiddle?
(Kadiddle, kadiddle, kadiddle,
Come dancing along down the middle . . .
Oh silly Kadiddle, Kadiddle!).

Hey diddle dinketty

Hey diddle dinketty, poppetty, pet!
The merchants of London they wear scarlet;
Silk in the collar, and gold in the hem,
So merrily march the merchantmen!

Sieve my lady's oatmeal

Sieve my lady's oatmeal,
Grind my lady's flour,
Put it in a chestnut,
Let it stand an hour –
One may rush, two may rush,
Come, my girls, walk under the bush.

Four-and-twenty tailors

Four-and-twenty tailors
Went to catch a snail,
The best man amongst them
Durst not touch her tail;
She put out her horns
Like a little kyloe cow,
Run, tailors, run!
Or she'll have you all e'en now!

Buz, quoth the blue fly

Buz, quoth the blue fly;
hum quoth the bee;
Buz and hum they cry,
and so do we!

In his ear, in his nose,
Thus do you see,
He ate the doormouse,
Else it was thee.

Once I saw a little bird

Once I saw a little bird
Come hop, hop, hop!
So I cried: 'Little bird,
Will you stop, stop, stop?'

And was going to the window
To say, 'How do you do?'
But he shook his little tail
And away he flew.

Three blind mice

Three blind mice, three blind mice,
See how they run!
They all run after the farmer's wife,
And she cut off their tails with a carving knife,
Did you ever see such a thing in your life
As three blind mice!

Pussy-cat sits by the fire

Pussy-cat sits by the fire;
How should she be fair?
In walks the little dog,
Says 'Pussy! are you there?

'How do you do, Mistress Pussy?
Mistress Pussy, how do you do?'
'I thank you kindly, little dog,
I fare as well as you!'

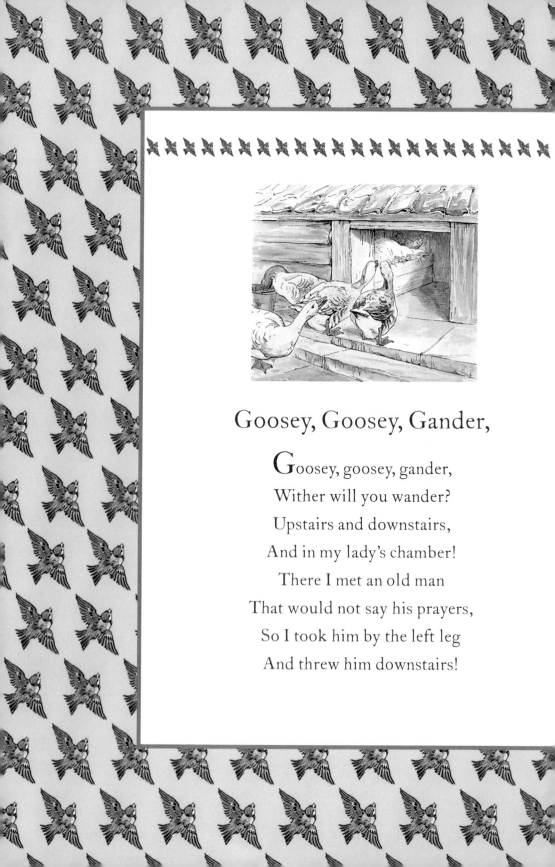

Goosey, Goosey, Gander,

Goosey, goosey, gander,
Wither will you wander?
Upstairs and downstairs,
And in my lady's chamber!
There I met an old man
That would not say his prayers,
So I took him by the left leg
And threw him downstairs!

Ninny Nanny Netticoat

Ninny Nanny Netticoat,
In a white petticoat,
With a red nose –
The longer she stands,
The shorter she grows.

What could this be?
Answer: A candle

We have a little garden

We have a little garden,
A garden of our own,
And every day we water there
The seeds that we have sown.

We love our little garden,
And tend it with such care,
You will not find a faded leaf
Or blighted blossom there.

This pig went to market

This pig went to market;
This pig stayed at home;
This pig had a bit of meat;
And this pig had none;
This little pig cried
'Wee! Wee! Wee!
I can't find my way home.'